MOTH
&
BUTTERFLY
TA-DA!

written by
Dev Petty

illustrated by
Ana Aranda

NANCY PAULSEN BOOKS

For Manya —D.P.

To my mother, the strongest person
I know, with all of my love —A.A.

NANCY PAULSEN BOOKS
An imprint of Penguin Random House LLC, New York

E
PETTY

$17.99   Visit us online at penguinrandomhouse.com

Library of Congress Cataloging-in-Publication Data is available.

Manufactured in China by RR Donnelley Asia Printing Solutions Ltd.

ISBN 9781524740511

SEP - 21   1 3 5 7 9 10 8 6 4 2

Design by Nicole Rheingans | Text set in Klepto ITC Std
The illustrations were done in watercolor, inks,
gouache, and lime on watercolor paper.

In a corner of the lush, green garden,
two caterpillars share a leaf.

They have a lot in common.

Many legs.

Spots.

And look! Both are champions
at chewing leaves into funny shapes.

Soon something important
will happen to each of them.

A week passes.

And another.

THEN...

POP!

There is Butterfly!

THEN...

POP

AGAIN!!!

There is Moth!

Wow, they have changed!
They have fewer legs now.
But they have antennae and . . . wings!

LOOK, MOTH,
MY WINGS ARE
SO BRIGHT!

At first, it is almost like before,
though now they drink sweet
nectar instead of chewing leaves.
And look! They can fly!

Moth and Butterfly,
together again.

But soon they notice other differences.
Butterfly is fast and graceful.

Moth darts around and bumps into everything.

Butterfly likes sunshine and standing out.
Moth loves shade and blending in.

MOTH?
WHERE ARE
YOU?

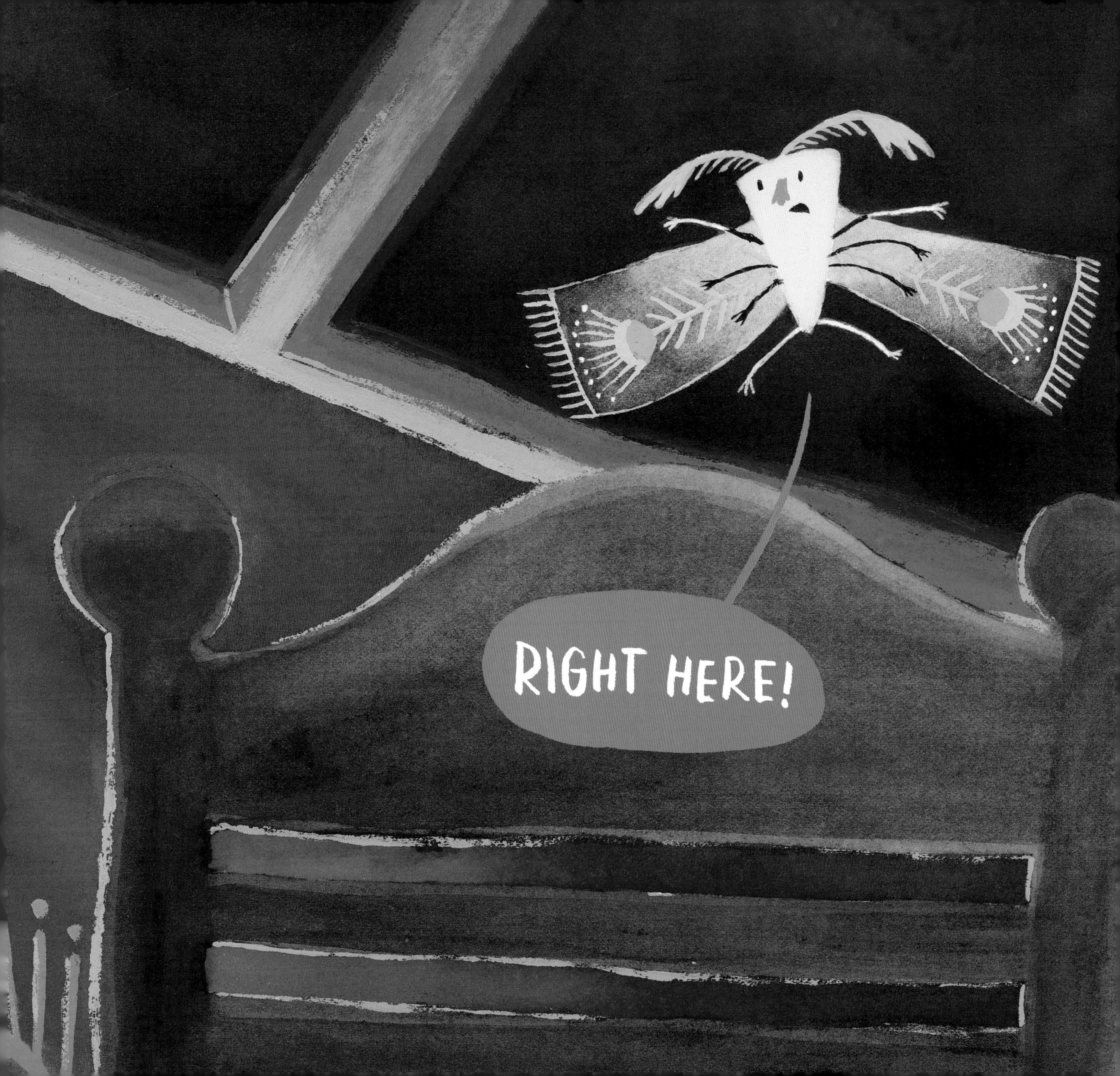
RIGHT HERE!

Butterfly flies in the daytime
and sleeps at night.

Moth sleeps in the day and flies at night.
He is waking up now.

Some things are different,
but some are the same.

Is it a moth or a butterfly?

You probably know that moths and butterflies have lots in common.
They both go through metamorphosis, the process that
turns them from a caterpillar into an amazing winged insect.

But there are easy ways to spot the differences after metamorphosis.
Butterflies are usually brightly colored and
have thin antennae with club-shaped tips.
Moths have duller colors and feathery antennae.
Another big difference between the two is that
butterflies are diurnal, meaning active in the daytime,
and moths are nocturnal, meaning they're busy during the night.

So go ahead and take a careful look
at those flying creatures—is it a moth or a butterfly?
Either way, they are both pretty grand, aren't they?